Aisha's New Look

by Catherine Murphy

illustrated by Janice Skivington

MODERN CURRICULUM PRESS

Pearson Learning Group

"Bug eyes!" I grumbled. "I've got space alien bug eyes!" I glared at the mirror. My reflected eyes glared back at me through the thick, shiny lenses of my brand-new glasses.

My mother stopped outside my door. "What did you say, Aisha?"

"Nothing. I'm fine," I said quickly.

My mother came in and asked, "Are you ready to go to Aunt Gail's?"

I dropped onto the bed. "I don't want to go, Mom."

My mother stared at me. "But Aisha, don't you want to see your cousin Danay?"

I nodded unhappily. "I do want to see Danay, Mom. But I don't want her to see me—not with these awful glasses."

My mother said, "Honey, your glasses aren't awful."

"Yes, they are!" I insisted.

My mother shook her head.

"They look fine. And they help you see."

I didn't like to admit it, but the glasses did help me see. Without the glasses, everything was just a blur. I'd been a resident of Bigford all my life, but until I got glasses, there were parts of my community I never saw.

Take leaves, for instance. Of course I knew that trees had leaves. But without the glasses, I couldn't see them clearly. They were a smudge, a blur. And birds! Before, I could hear birds chirping, but I never saw them in focus, except in books. Now I saw birds everywhere—in the trees, on the roofs, and on the wires strung across our street.

I liked the way the world looked through my glasses, but I didn't like the way I looked wearing them. That was the part my mother didn't understand.

Little kids look cute in glasses. Grown-up women look smart in fashion frames. But I was at that in-between age when glasses just look bad.

My mom patted me on the shoulder. "Let's go see my sister and your cousin, and let's have a good time."

For the whole ride to Aunt Gail's, I worried. I didn't see Danay very often. She lived in Clifton, the community where my mom and aunt grew up. My mom and dad had moved away, but Aunt Gail was still a Clifton resident.

Usually, I loved visiting Aunt Gail, because Danay wasn't just my cousin. She also was my good friend. But now I had the glasses. Maybe Danay wouldn't like the new me.

When we arrived, Aunt Gail came running out to greet my mother.

"Come on in, honey," Aunt Gail called to me. "Have some cheesecake!"

They went inside to find Uncle Joe. I stayed in the car. I just didn't feel ready to face Danay with glasses on my face.

Finally, Danay came outside to find me.
Her brown eyes looked so big and pretty.
Before she got to the car, I yanked my glasses
off and hid them in my pocket.

When I climbed out of the car, my cousin
didn't grin at me the way she usually did.
Instead, she looked worried, and she didn't
smile at all.

"Hey, Aisha," she said, looking away from
me. I was confused. Had she seen my glasses
after all? What was wrong?

As soon as we got inside, my mother said firmly, "Put those glasses right back on, Aisha. You've got to wear them, or your eyes won't adjust."

Danay turned to stare at me. "Glasses? What glasses?" she asked.

I took a deep breath, pulled the glasses out of my pocket, and slid them on. Before Danay could say anything, I looked over her shoulder and gasped.

Through the picture window behind Danay, I could see a baby girl, not even two years old. She was playing near the street. Then, as I stared, she toddled into the road.

"No!" I yelled with horror.

I ran out the door and across the yard. As I dashed toward her, the baby squatted down to pick up a shiny pebble in the road.

I could hear the sound of a car rushing toward us. My heart pounded as I jumped off the curb and ran into the street.

Brakes squealed. A car swerved. Just in time, I grabbed the little girl and lifted her into my arms.

My family ran up to us. The baby's panicked mother came running out of the house next door. Everybody hugged the little girl and me, and cried.

Finally, the grown-ups took the little girl inside, leaving me and Danay in the yard.

"You saved that baby's life, Aisha," Danay said. "It's so lucky you got those glasses. You might not have seen her without them!"

I was surprised. "I didn't think of that."

Danay smiled at me. Between her lips, something metal glittered.

"Hey!" I said. "When did you get braces?"

"Yesterday." Danay made a face. "I was afraid to let you see them before. I think they look so dumb."

I couldn't believe it. "That's what I thought about my glasses!" I said. "But your braces don't look dumb at all."

We stared at each other for a second. Then we both started to laugh.

"Your glasses don't look dumb, either. Do you want some cheesecake?" Danay asked.

"Great idea," I said. But before we went inside, I stopped for just a minute to polish my new glasses. I wanted to make sure that I could see every single thing a person might ever want to see, in the whole wide beautiful world.